Oksana Deimak.

P9-CAE-945

Welcome to a Tale of Asgard...

Thor, the prince of Asgard, is a brash and impetuous youth. Never one to consider who he is or what he has, Thor's mind is always on who he will one day be and what the future holds for him. He feels he lives in the shadow of his father, Odin, ruler of all Asgard, and hopes he can escape that fate through noble deeds and valiant acts.

In order to prove himself worthy of the destiny he covets, Thor sneaks into the imperial armory with his friends, Balder and Sif. Legend holds that whoever can lift the mighty Uru hammer, Mjolnir, will possess great power. But, try as he might, Thor cannot budge the hammer. Before he and his friends can sneak away from their failure, Thor's jealous half-brother, Loki, transforms three spiders into gargantuan arachnid beasts and unleashes them on the trio.

Working as a team, Thor and his friends use the weapons around them to defeat their eight-legged foes. Fearing punishment for their actions, the teens are surprised to win praise from Odin himself for their heroics in battle. Having now proven themselves accomplished warriors, Odin asks the valiant youths to undertake a quest on his behalf: they must travel Asgard in search of four mystic elements that he will use to forge an enchanted sword. Without consulting Balder or Sif, Thor brashly accepts the quest on their behalf, which does not sit well with the young warriors.

It is with mixed emotions that Thor, Balder and Sif set out on Odin's Quest in search of the first element their liege requires... a scale from the hide of the dragon, Hakurei!

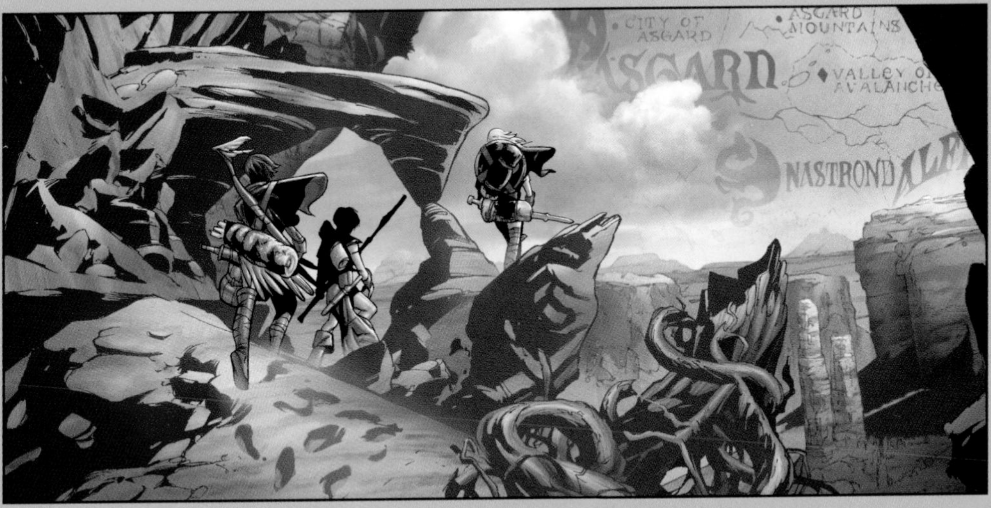

CITY OF ASGARD
ASGARD MOUNTAINS
NASTROND

Part Two

The Heat of Hakurei

Akira Yoshida
WRITER

Greg Tocchini
PENCILER

Jay Leisten
INKER

Guru eFX
COLORIST

VC's Randy Gentile
LETTERER

Adi Granov
COVER ARTIST

MacKenzie Cadenhead
EDITOR

Ralph Macchio & C.B. Cebulski
CONSULTING EDITORS

Joe Quesada
EDITOR IN CHIEF

Dan Buckley
PUBLISHER

MARVEL

Spotlight

VISIT US AT
www.abdopublishing.com

Reinforced library bound edition published in 2007 by Spotlight, a division of the ABDO Publishing Group, Edina, Minnesota. Spotlight produces high quality reinforced library bound editions for schools and libraries. Published by agreement with Marvel Characters, Inc.

MARVEL, and all related character names and the distinctive likenesses thereof are trademarks of Marvel Characters, Inc., and is/are used with permission. Copyright © 2007 Marvel Characters, Inc. All rights reserved. www.marvel.com

MARVEL, Thor, Son of Asgard: TM & © 2004 Marvel Characters, Inc. All rights reserved. www.marvel.com. This book is produced under license from Marvel Characters, Inc.

Library of Congress Cataloging-in-Publication Data

Yoshida, Akira.
   Thor, son of Asgard / [Akira Yoshida, writer ; Greg Tocchini, penciler ; Jay Leisten, inker ; Guru e FX, colorist ; Adi Granov, cover artist ; Randy Gentile, letterer].
      p. cm.
   Cover title.
   "Marvel Age."
   Revisions of issues 1-6 of the serial Thor, son of Asgard.
   Contents: pt. 1. The warriors teen -- pt. 2. The heat of Hakurei -- pt. 3. The nest of Gnori -- pt. 4. The jaws of Jennia -- pt. 5. The lake of Lilitha -- pt. 6. The trio triumphant.
      ISBN-13: 978-1-59961-286-7 (pt. 1)
      ISBN-10: 1-59961-286-0 (pt. 1)
      ISBN-13: 978-1-59961-287-4 (pt. 2)
      ISBN-10: 1-59961-287-9 (pt. 2)
      ISBN-13: 978-1-59961-288-1 (pt. 3)
      ISBN-10: 1-59961-288-7 (pt. 3)
      ISBN-13: 978-1-59961-289-8 (pt. 4)
      ISBN-10: 1-59961-289-5 (pt. 4)
      ISBN-13: 978-1-59961-290-4 (pt. 5)
      ISBN-10: 1-59961-290-9 (pt. 5)
      ISBN-13: 978-1-59961-291-1 (pt. 6)
      ISBN-10: 1-59961-291-7 (pt. 6)
   1. Comic books, strips, etc. I. Tocchini, Greg. II. Title. III. Title: Warriors teen. IV. Title: Heat of Hakurei. V. Title: Nest of Gnori. VI. Title: Jaws of Jennia. VII. Title: Lake of Lilitha. VIII. Title: Trio triumphant.

PN6728.T64Y68 2007
791.5'73--dc22

                      2006050635

All Spotlight books are reinforced library binding and manufactured in the United States of America.

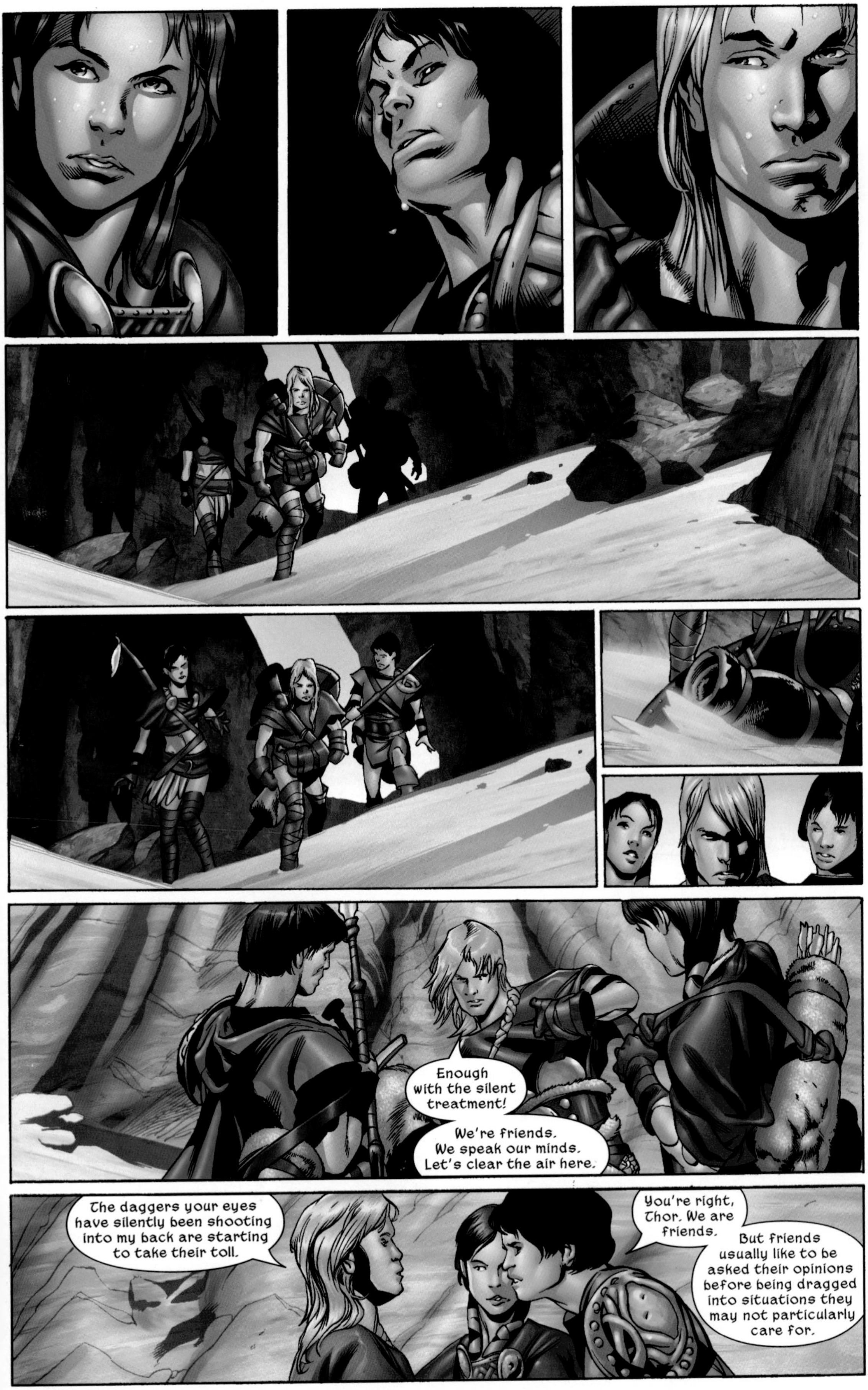
Enough with the silent treatment!
We're friends. We speak our minds. Let's clear the air here.
The daggers your eyes have silently been shooting into my back are starting to take their toll.
You're right, Thor. We are friends.
But friends usually like to be asked their opinions before being dragged into situations they may not particularly care for.

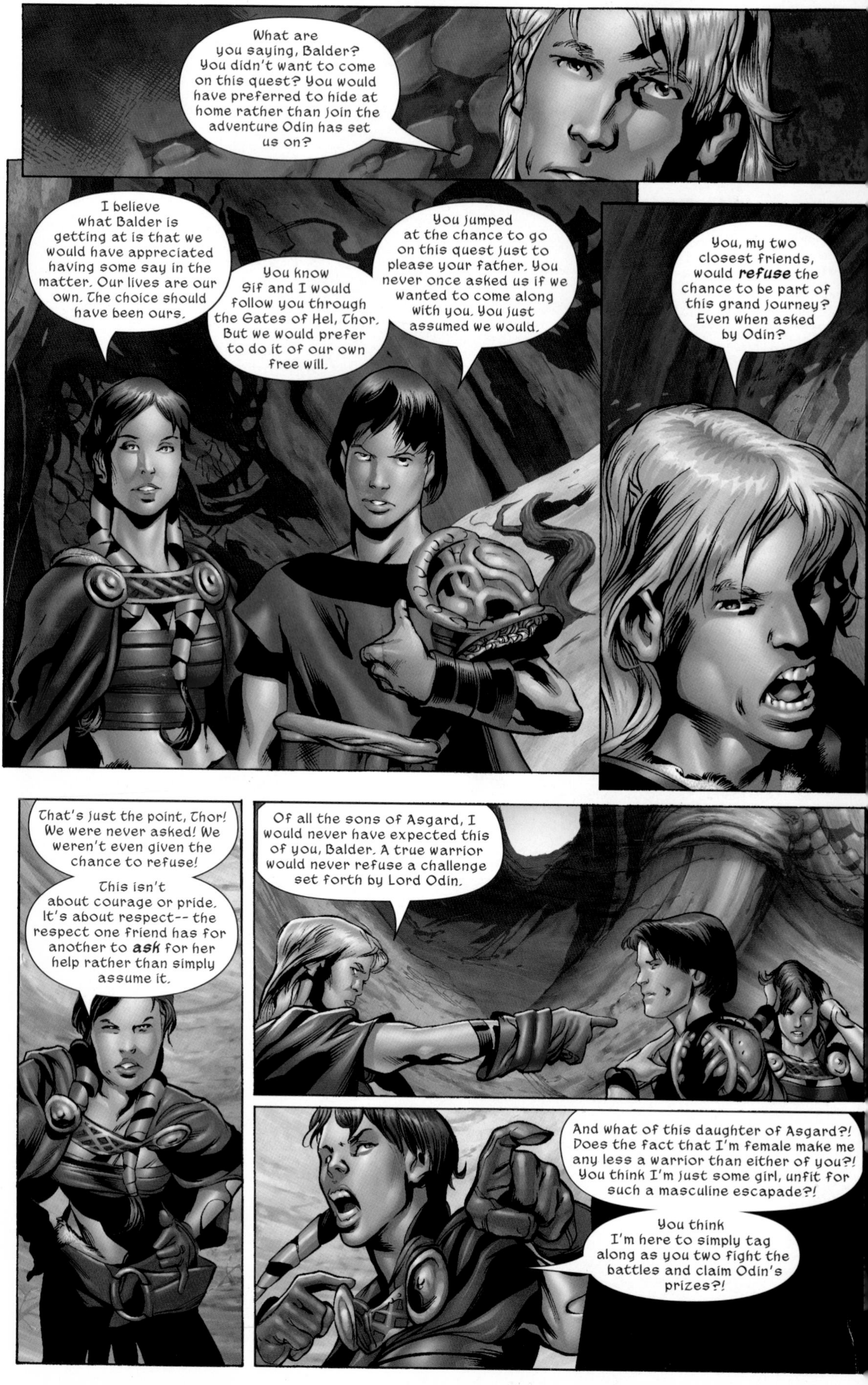
What are you saying, Balder? You didn't want to come on this quest? You would have preferred to hide at home rather than join the adventure Odin has set us on?
I believe what Balder is getting at is that we would have appreciated having some say in the matter. Our lives are our own. The choice should have been ours.
You know Sif and I would follow you through the Gates of Hel, Thor. But we would prefer to do it of our own free will.
You jumped at the chance to go on this quest just to please your father. You never once asked us if we wanted to come along with you. You just assumed we would.
You, my two closest friends, would refuse the chance to be part of this grand journey? Even when asked by Odin?
That's just the point, Thor! We were never asked! We weren't even given the chance to refuse!
This isn't about courage or pride. It's about respect-- the respect one friend has for another to ask for her help rather than simply assume it.
Of all the sons of Asgard, I would never have expected this of you, Balder. A true warrior would never refuse a challenge set forth by Lord Odin.
And what of this daughter of Asgard?! Does the fact that I'm female make me any less a warrior than either of you?! You think I'm just some girl, unfit for such a masculine escapade?!
You think I'm here to simply tag along as you two fight the battles and claim Odin's prizes?!

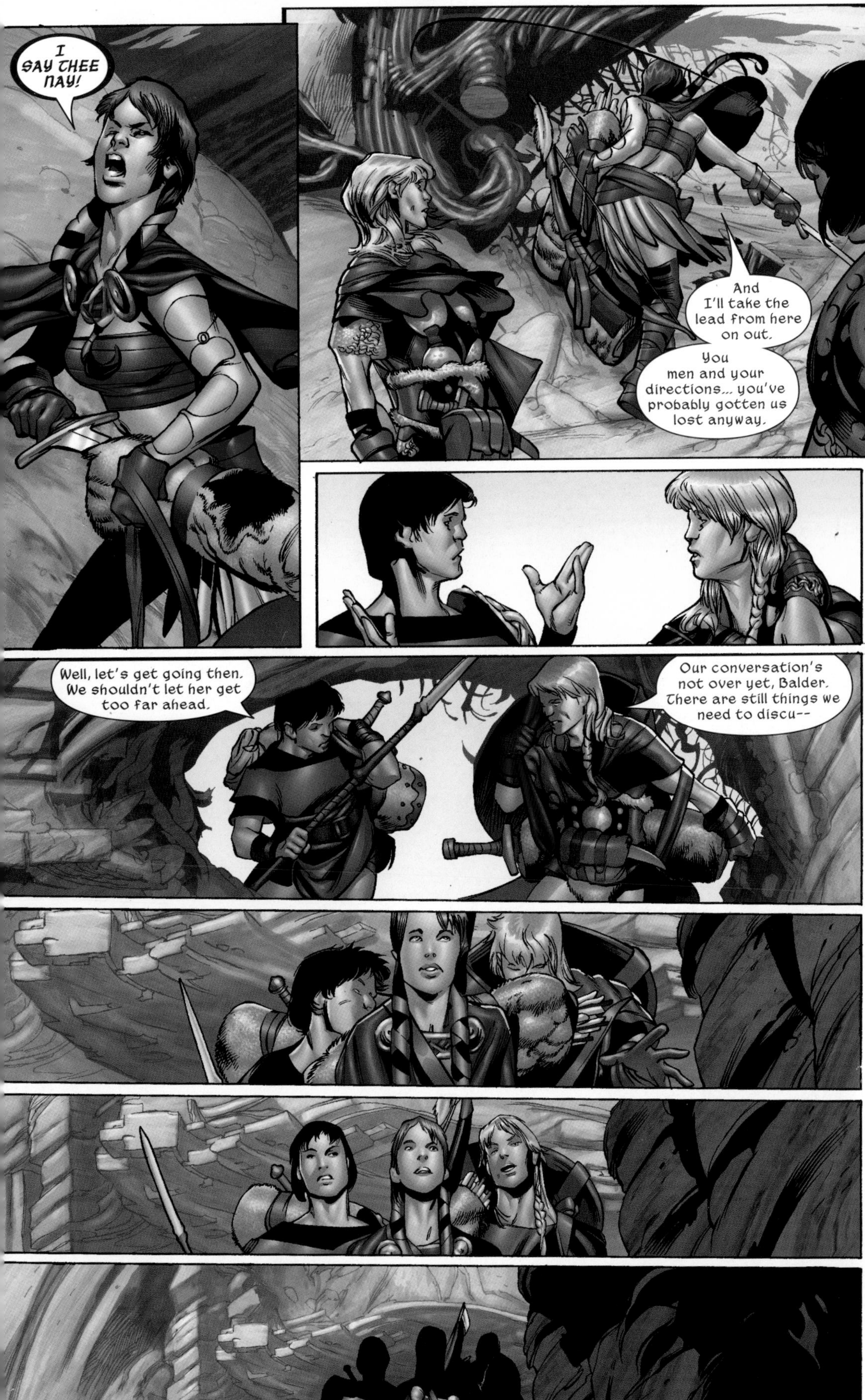
I SAY THEE NAY!
And I'll take the lead from here on out.
You men and your directions... you've probably gotten us lost anyway.
Well, let's get going then. We shouldn't let her get too far ahead.
Our conversation's not over yet, Balder. There are still things we need to discu--

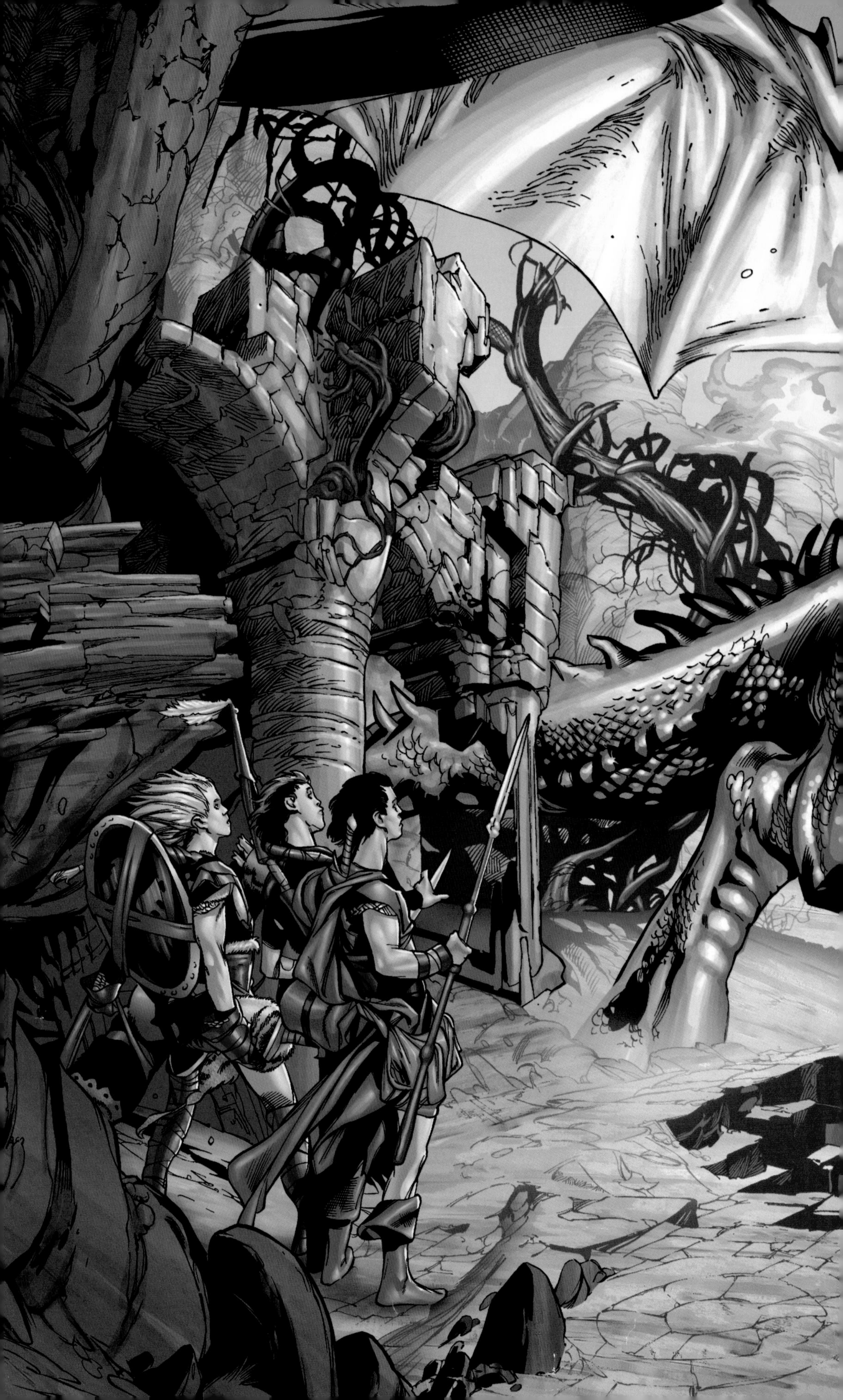

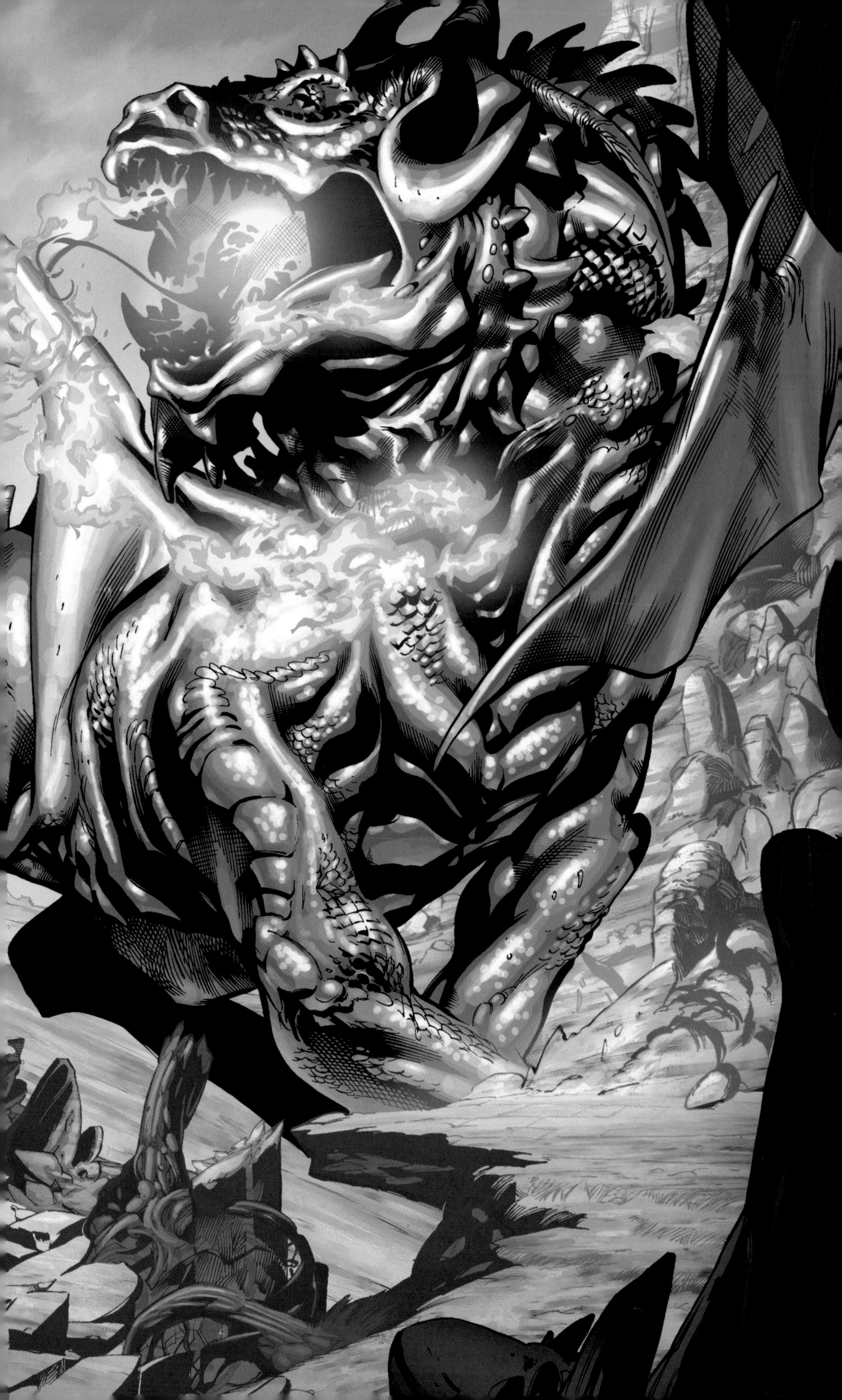

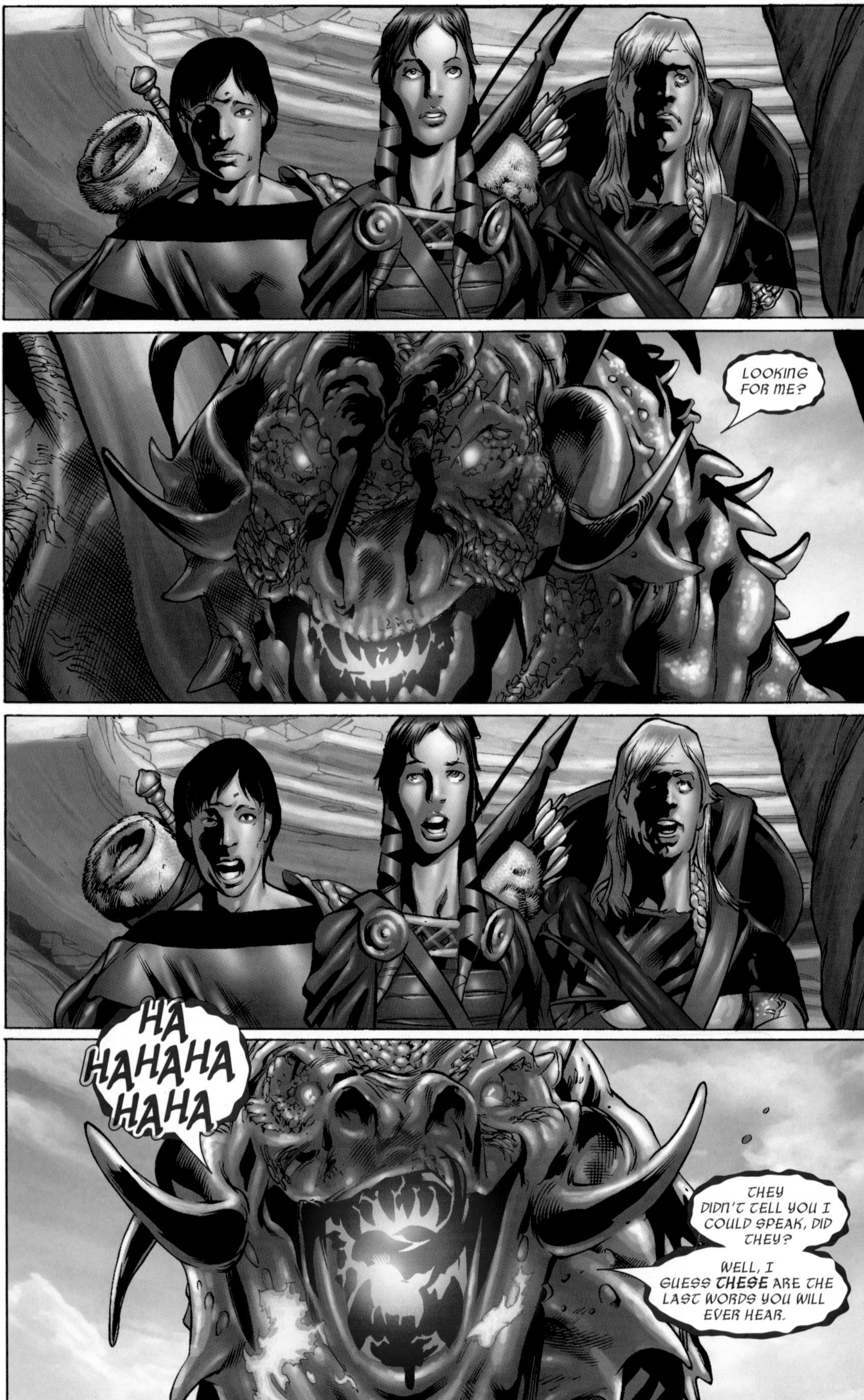
LOOKING FOR ME?
HA HAHAHA HAHA
THEY DIDN'T TELL YOU I COULD SPEAK, DID THEY?
WELL, I GUESS **THESE** ARE THE LAST WORDS YOU WILL EVER HEAR.

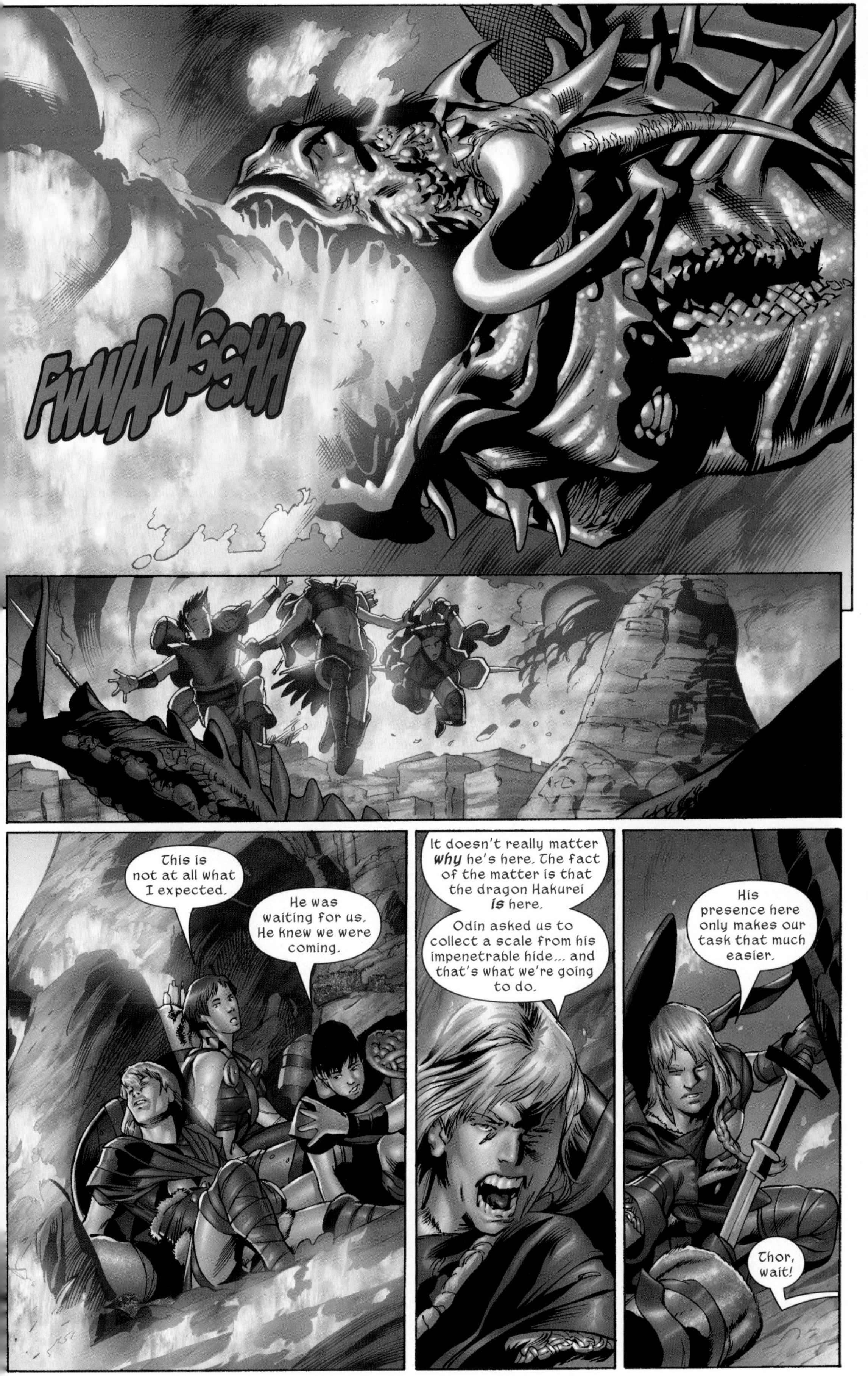
FWWAASSHH
This is not at all what I expected.
He was waiting for us. He knew we were coming.
It doesn't really matter **why** he's here. The fact of the matter is that the dragon Hakurei **is** here.
Odin asked us to collect a scale from his impenetrable hide... and that's what we're going to do.
His presence here only makes our task that much easier.
Thor, wait!

I am Thor, Son of Odin!

On behalf of my father, ruler of all Asgard, I command you to cease your attack and comply with my requests!

I KNOW WHO YOU ARE, YOU NAIVE, YOUNG WHELP.

IT IS **YOU** WHO HAVE NO IDEA WHO YOU ARE DEALING WITH!

WWHOOOSSSHH

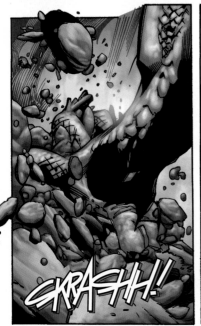

SKRASHH!

Sif! Balder!

We're all right. Turn your attention back to the dragon!

Thor! Look out!

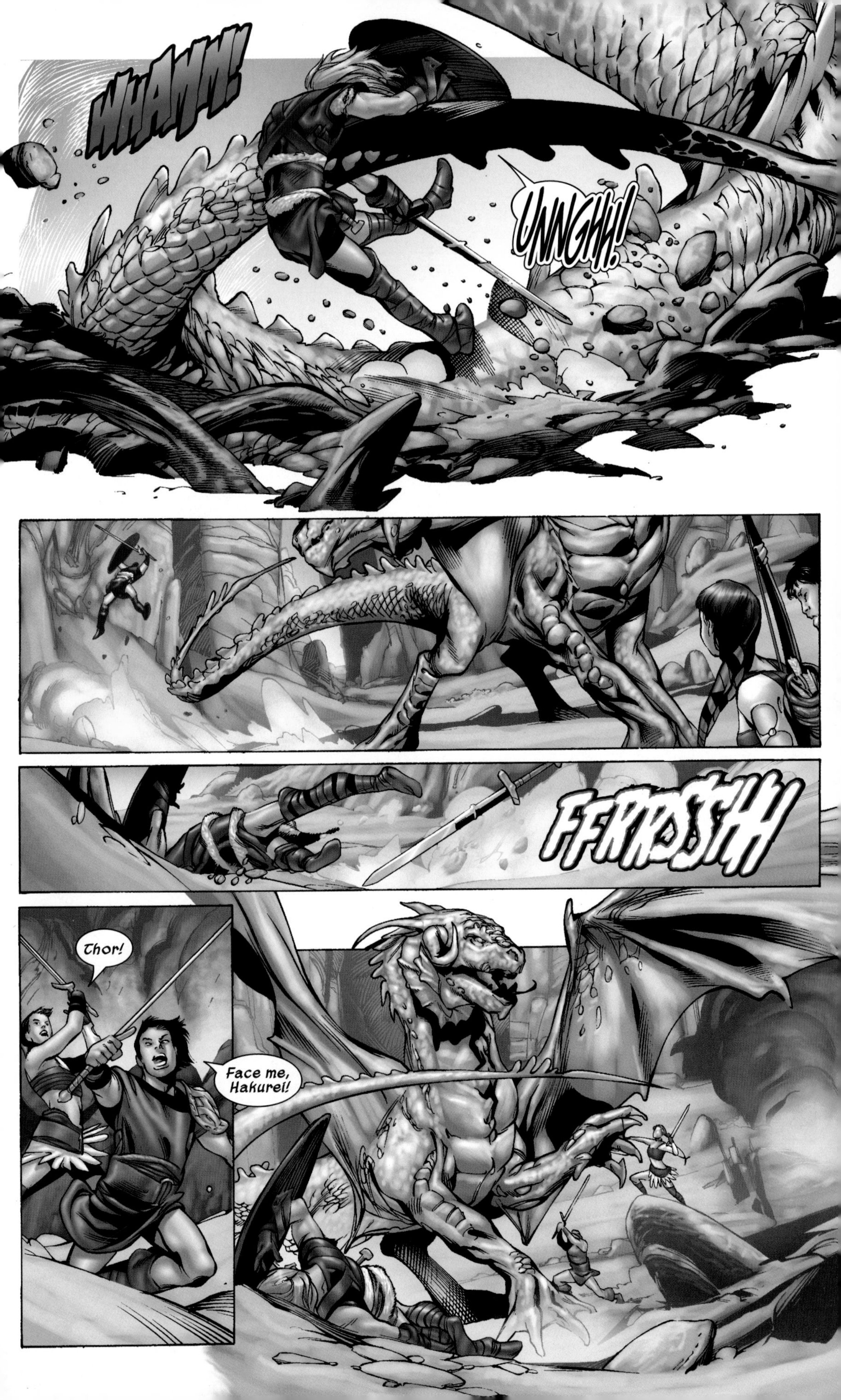

WHAMM!
UNNGHH!
FFRRSSHH
Thor!
Face me, Hakurei!

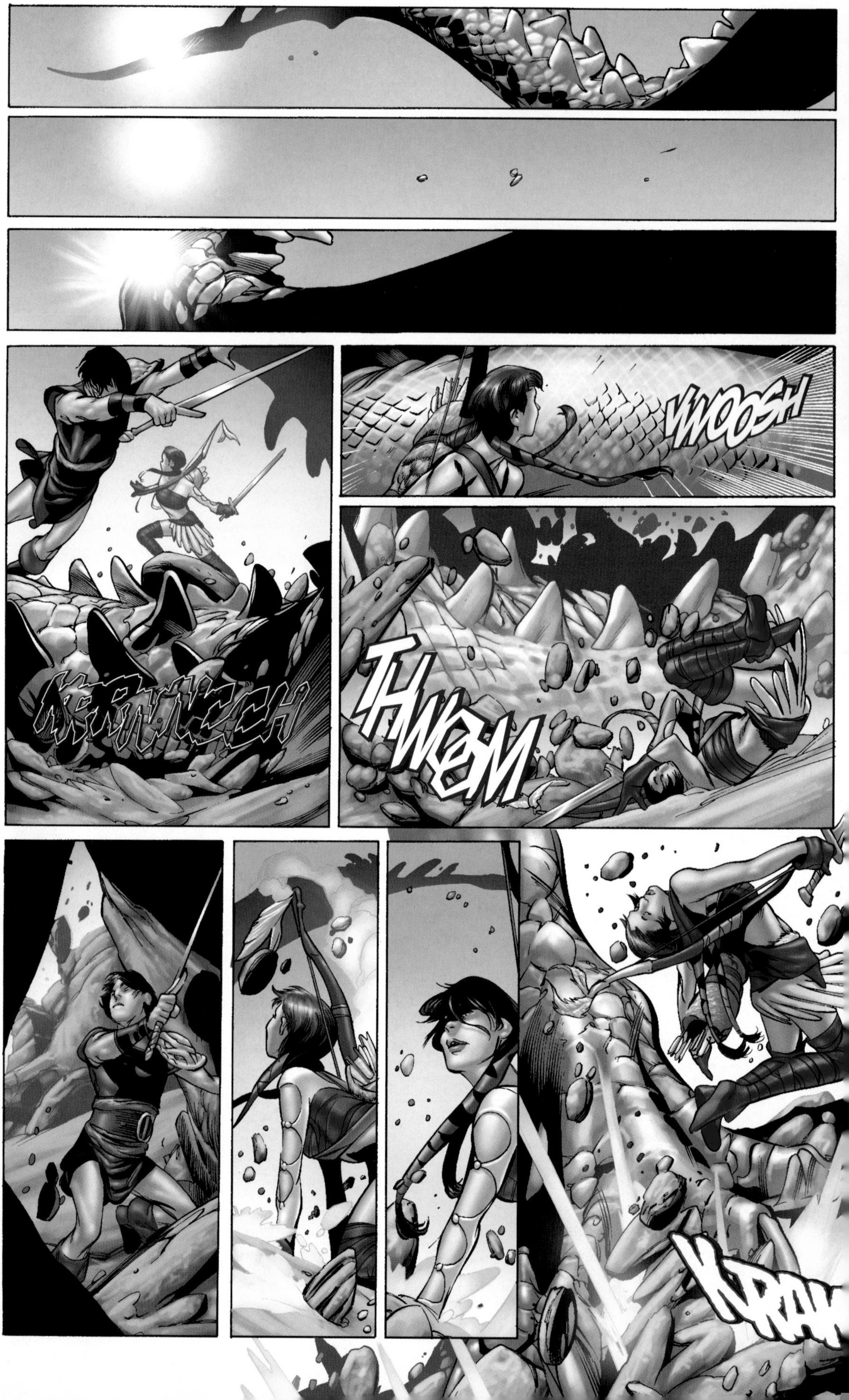
WOOSH
KRRUNCH
THWOOM

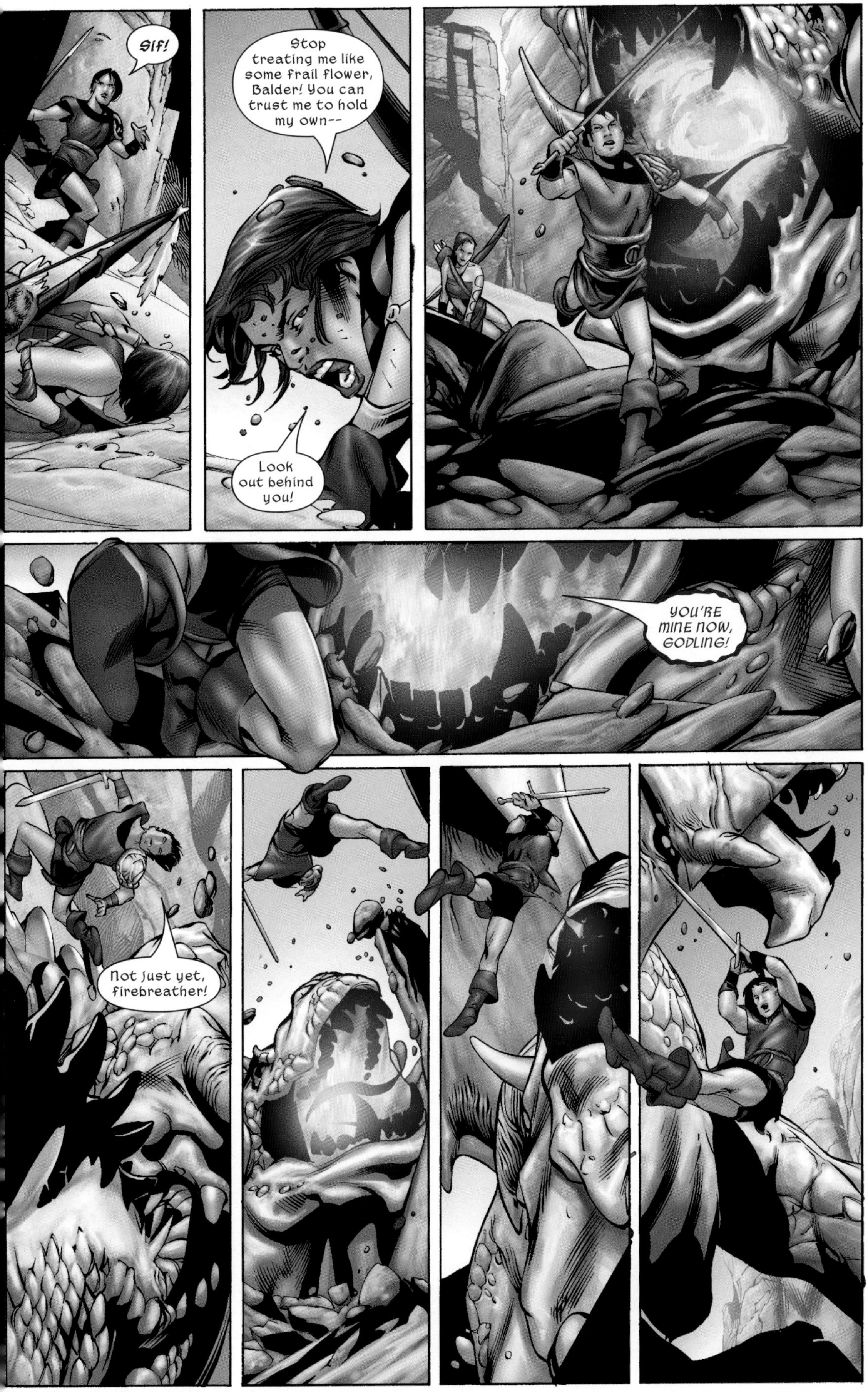
Sif!
Stop treating me like some frail flower, Balder! You can trust me to hold my own--
Look out behind you!
YOU'RE MINE NOW, GODLING!
Not just yet, firebreather!

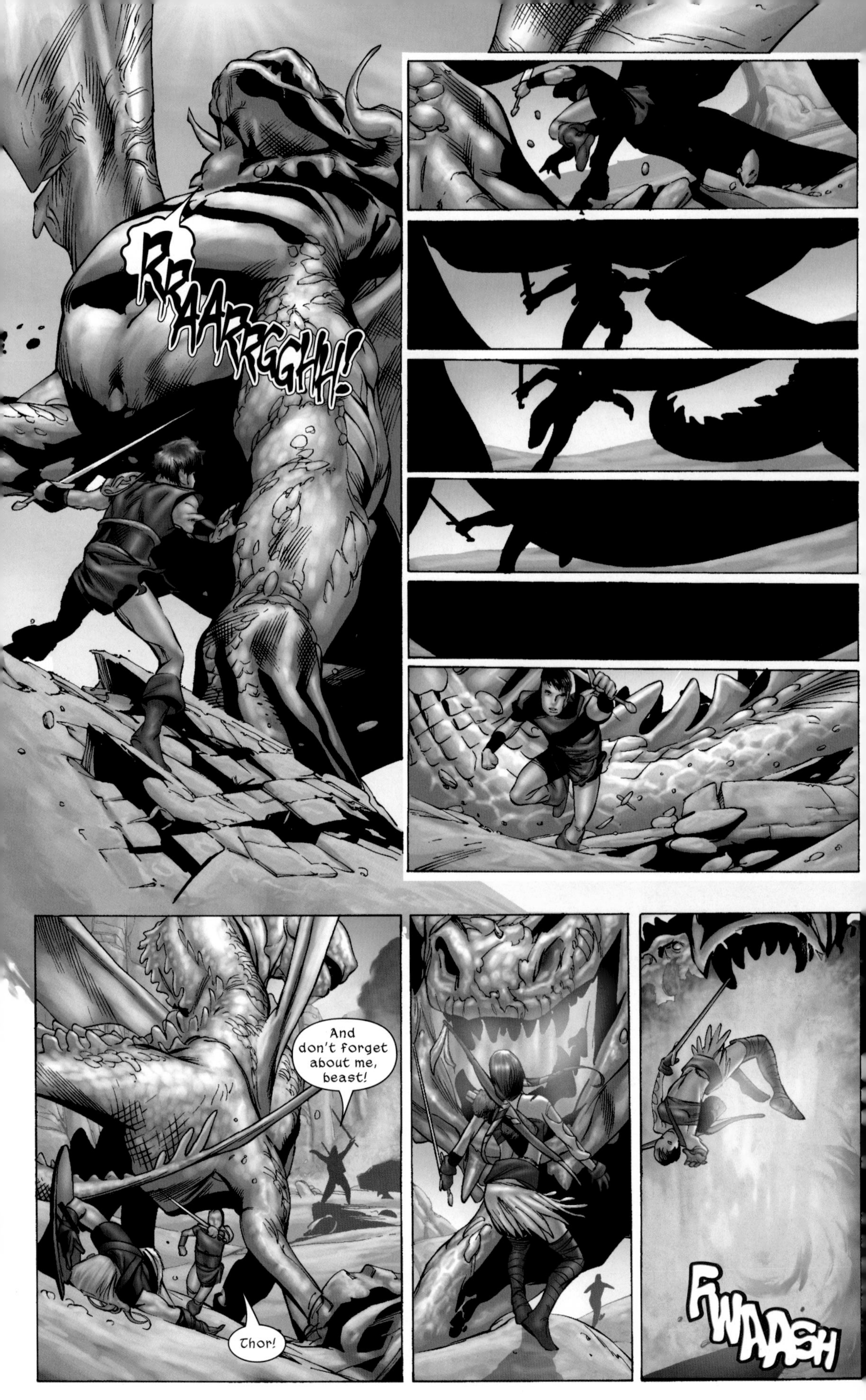
RRAARRGGHH!
And don't forget about me, beast!
Thor!
FWAASH

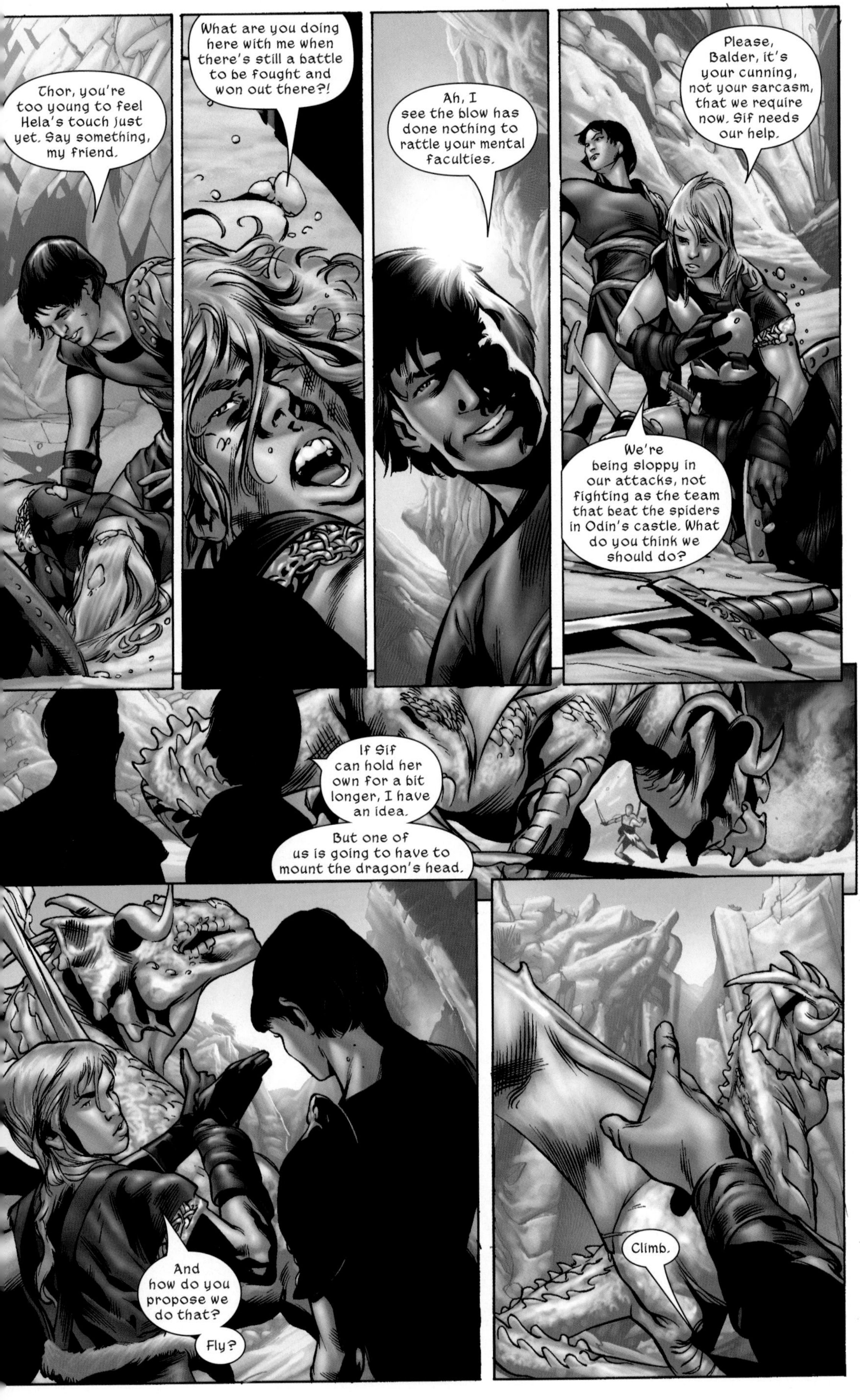
Thor, you're too young to feel Hela's touch just yet. Say something, my friend.
What are you doing here with me when there's still a battle to be fought and won out there?!
Ah, I see the blow has done nothing to rattle your mental faculties.
Please, Balder, it's your cunning, not your sarcasm, that we require now. Sif needs our help.
We're being sloppy in our attacks, not fighting as the team that beat the spiders in Odin's castle. What do you think we should do?
If Sif can hold her own for a bit longer, I have an idea.
But one of us is going to have to mount the dragon's head.
And how do you propose we do that?
Fly?
Climb.

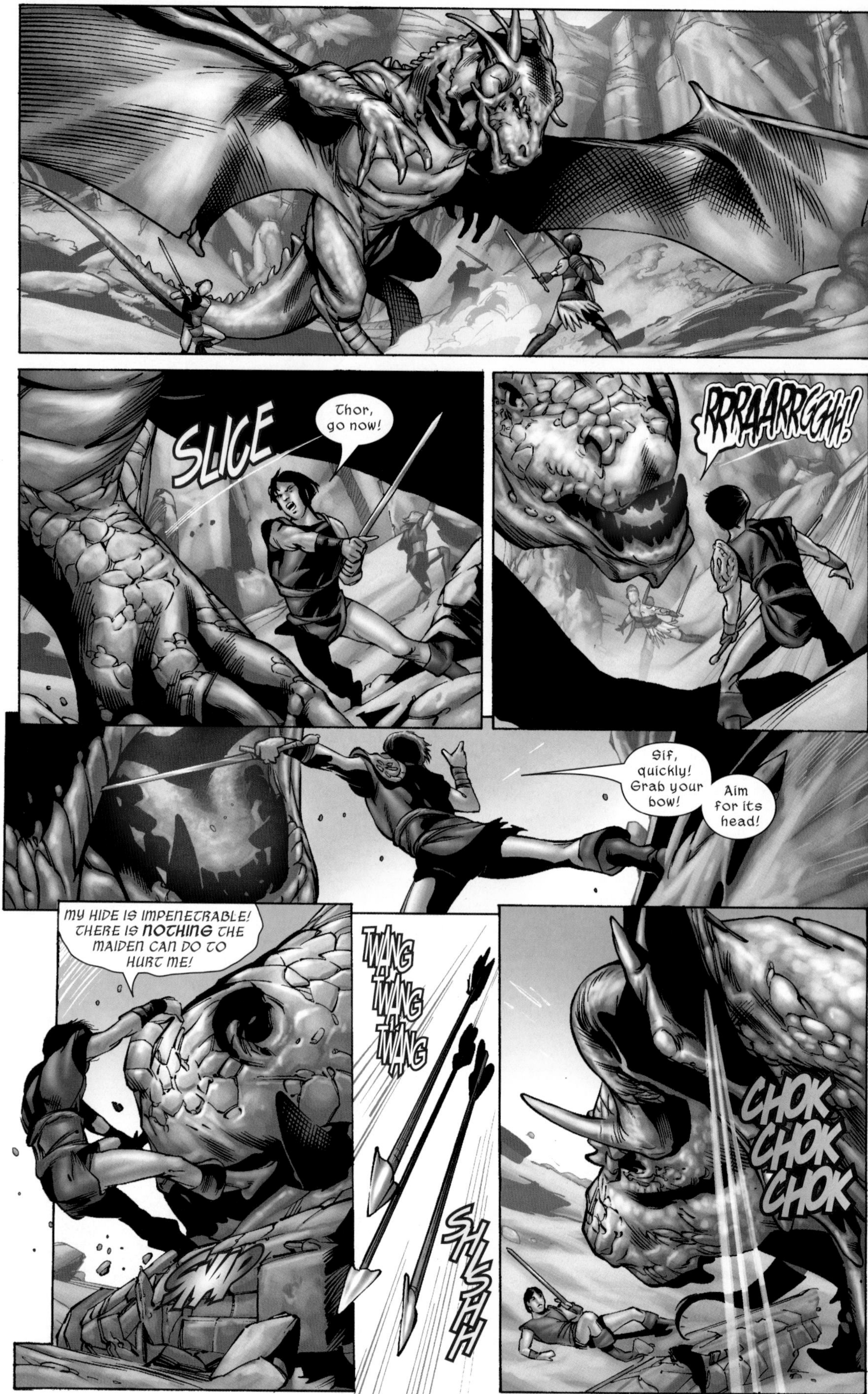
SLICE
Thor, go now!
RRRAARRGGHH!
Sif, quickly! Grab your bow!
Aim for its head!
MY HIDE IS IMPENETRABLE! THERE IS NOTHING THE MAIDEN CAN DO TO HURT ME!
TWANG TWANG TWANG
SHSHSHH
CHOK CHOK CHOK

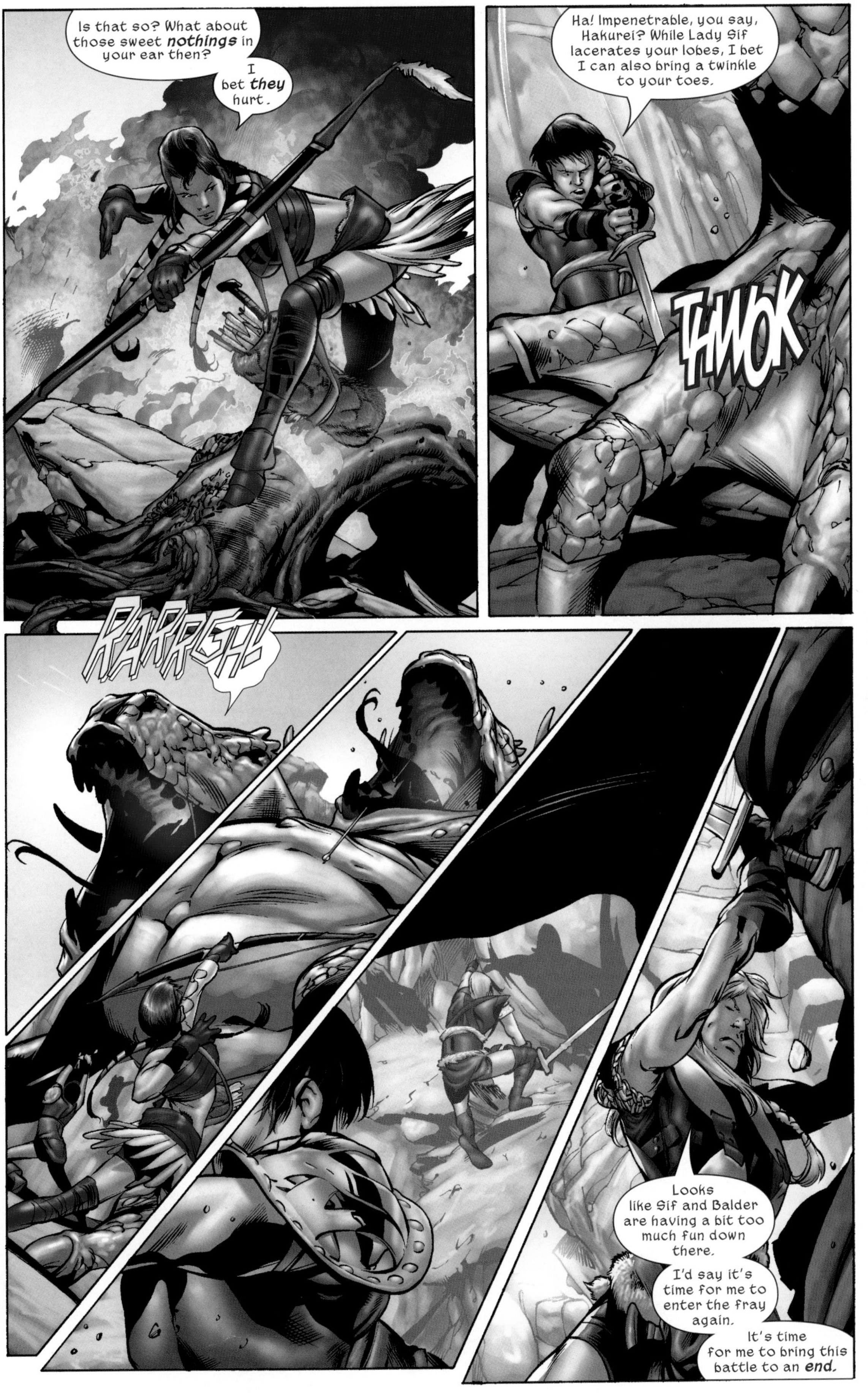

Is that so? What about those sweet *nothings* in your ear then?
I bet *they* hurt.
Ha! Impenetrable, you say, Hakurei? While Lady Sif lacerates your lobes, I bet I can also bring a twinkle to your toes.
THWOK
RARRGH!
Looks like Sif and Balder are having a bit too much fun down there.
I'd say it's time for me to enter the fray again.
It's time for me to bring this battle to an *end.*

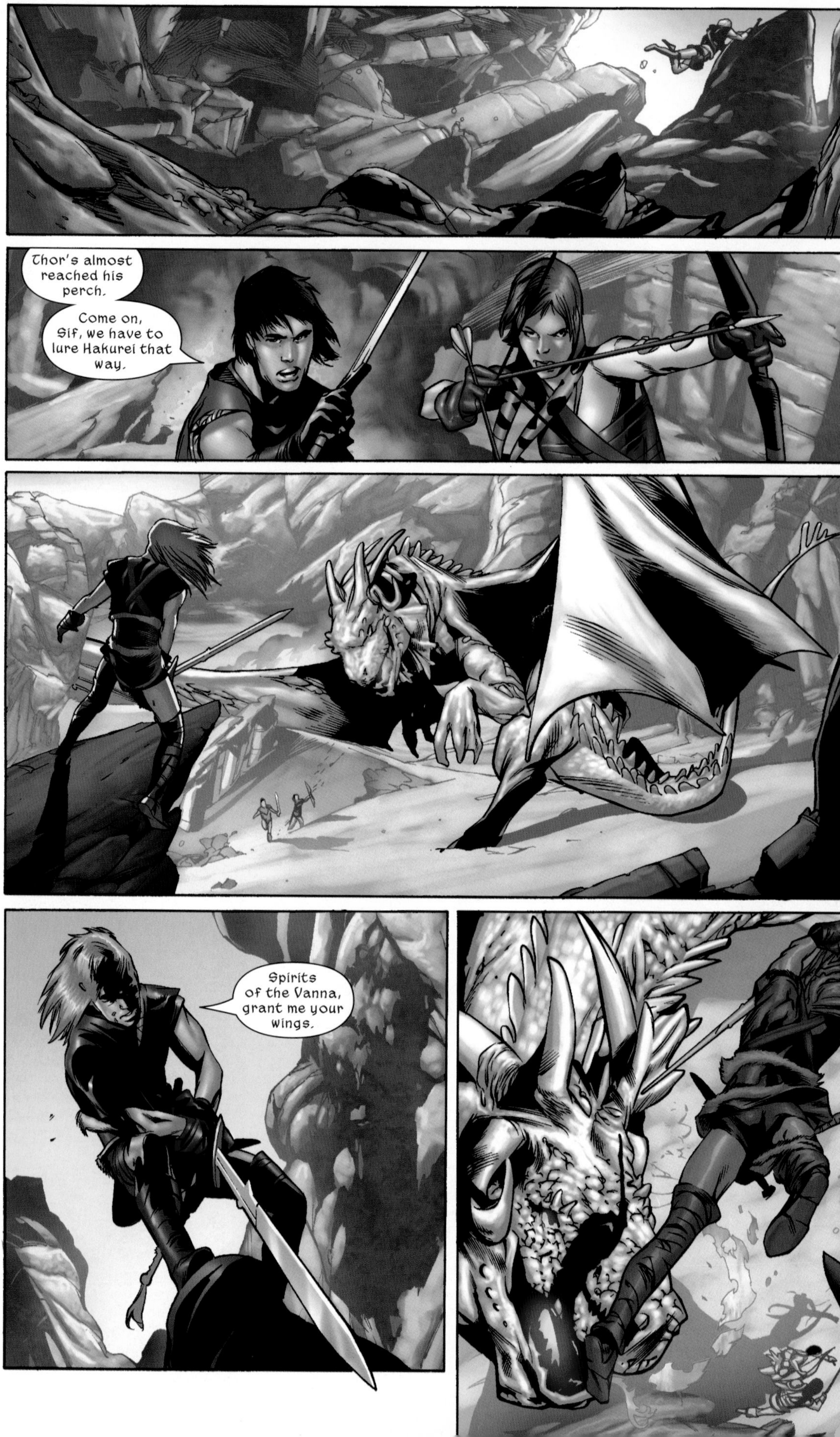
Thor's almost reached his perch.
Come on, Sif, we have to lure Hakurei that way.
Spirits of the Vanna, grant me your wings.

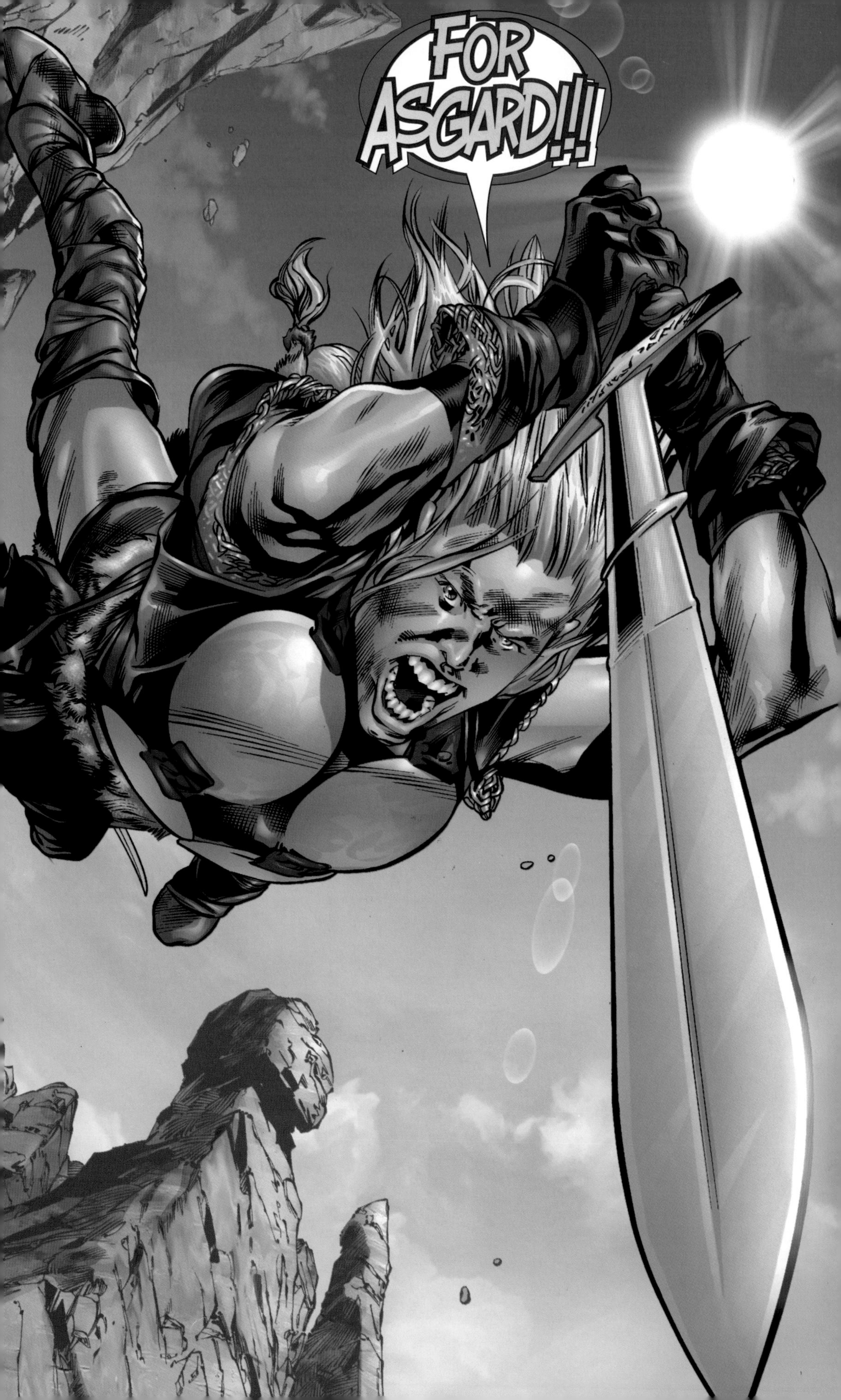
FOR ASGARD!!!

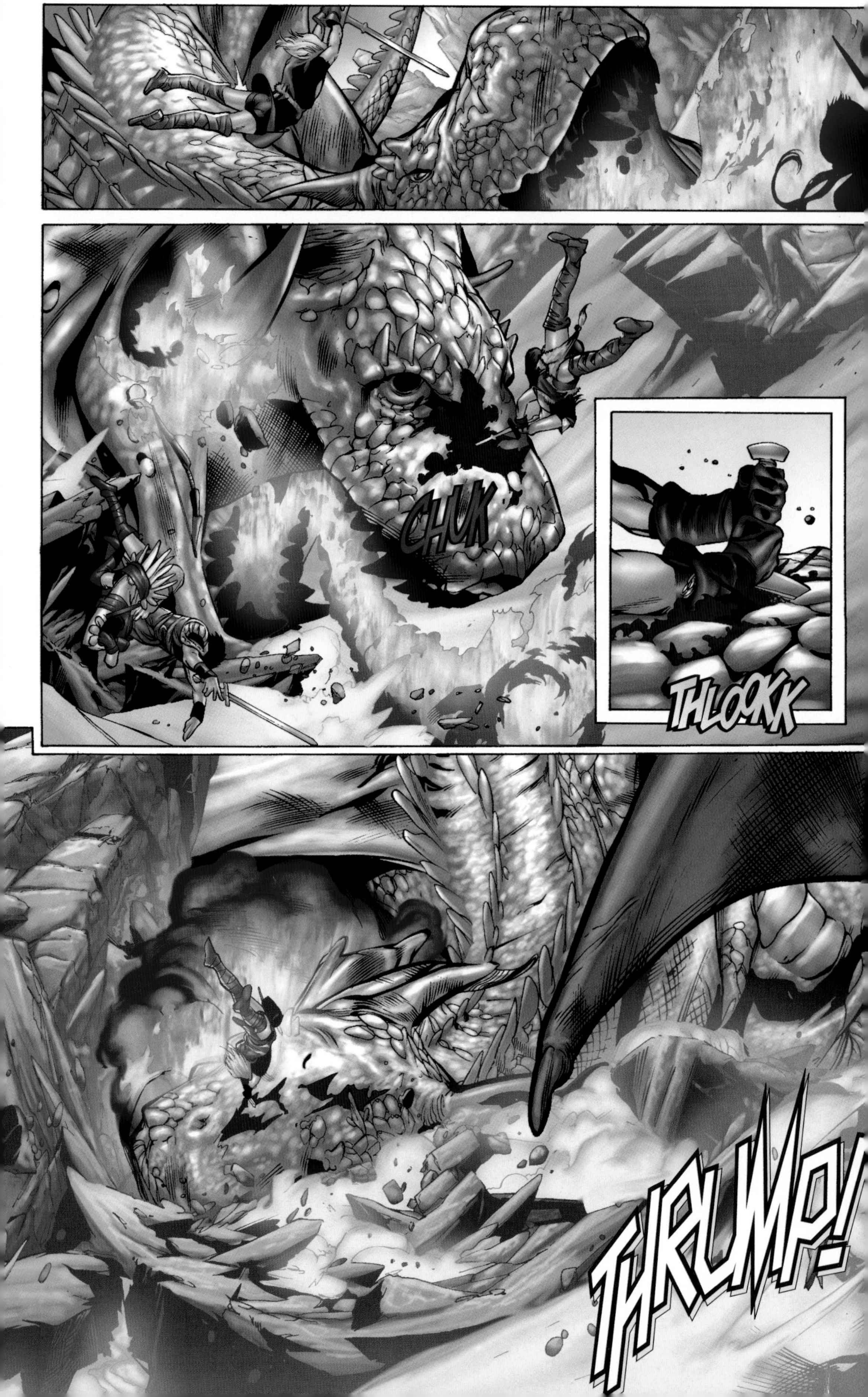
CHUK
THLOOKK
THRUMP!

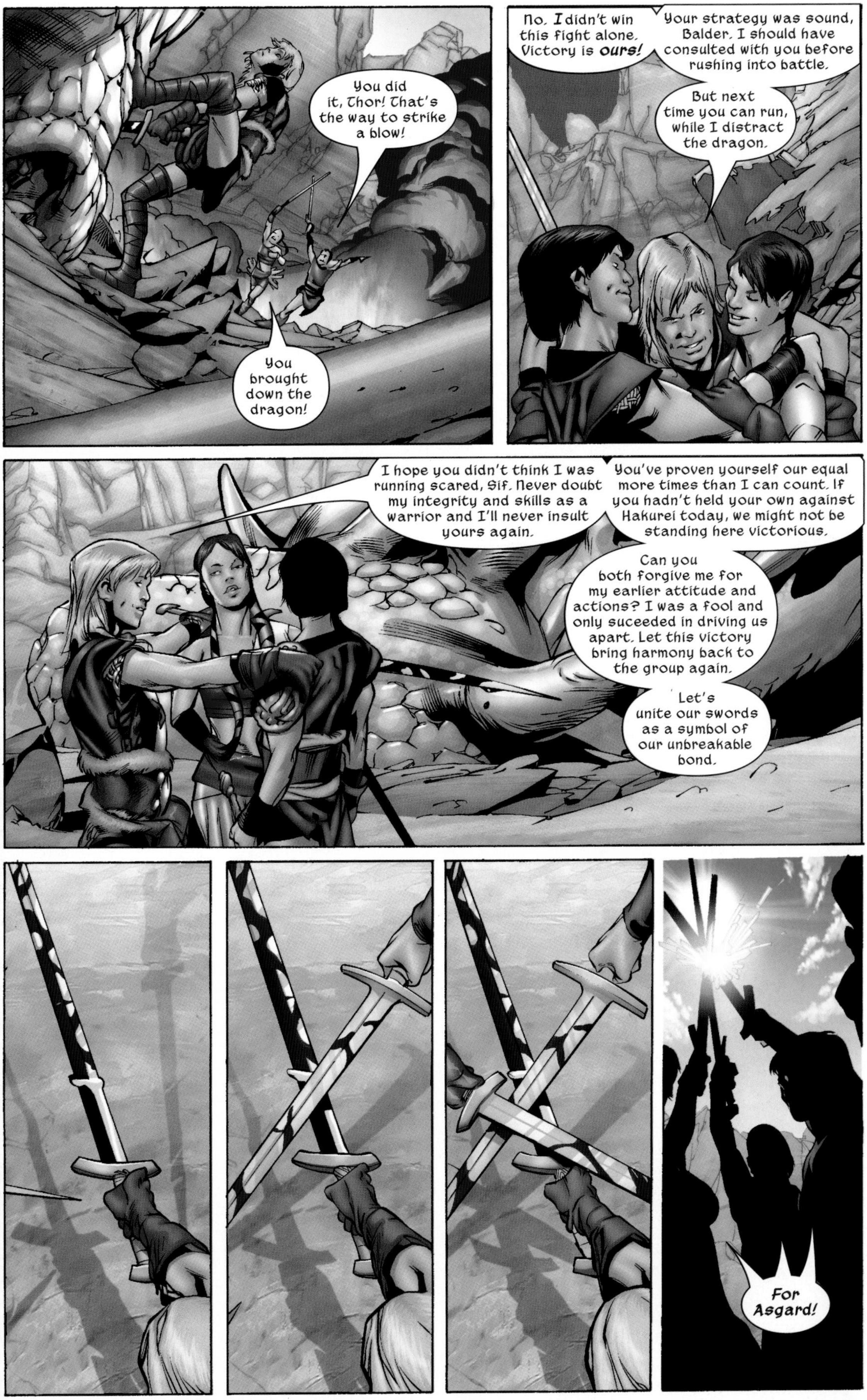
You did it, Thor! That's the way to strike a blow!
You brought down the dragon!
No, I didn't win this fight alone. Victory is ours!
Your strategy was sound, Balder. I should have consulted with you before rushing into battle.
But next time you can run, while I distract the dragon.
I hope you didn't think I was running scared, Sif. Never doubt my integrity and skills as a warrior and I'll never insult yours again.
You've proven yourself our equal more times than I can count. If you hadn't held your own against Hakurei today, we might not be standing here victorious.
Can you both forgive me for my earlier attitude and actions? I was a fool and only suceeded in driving us apart. Let this victory bring harmony back to the group again.
Let's unite our swords as a symbol of our unbreakable bond.
For Asgard!

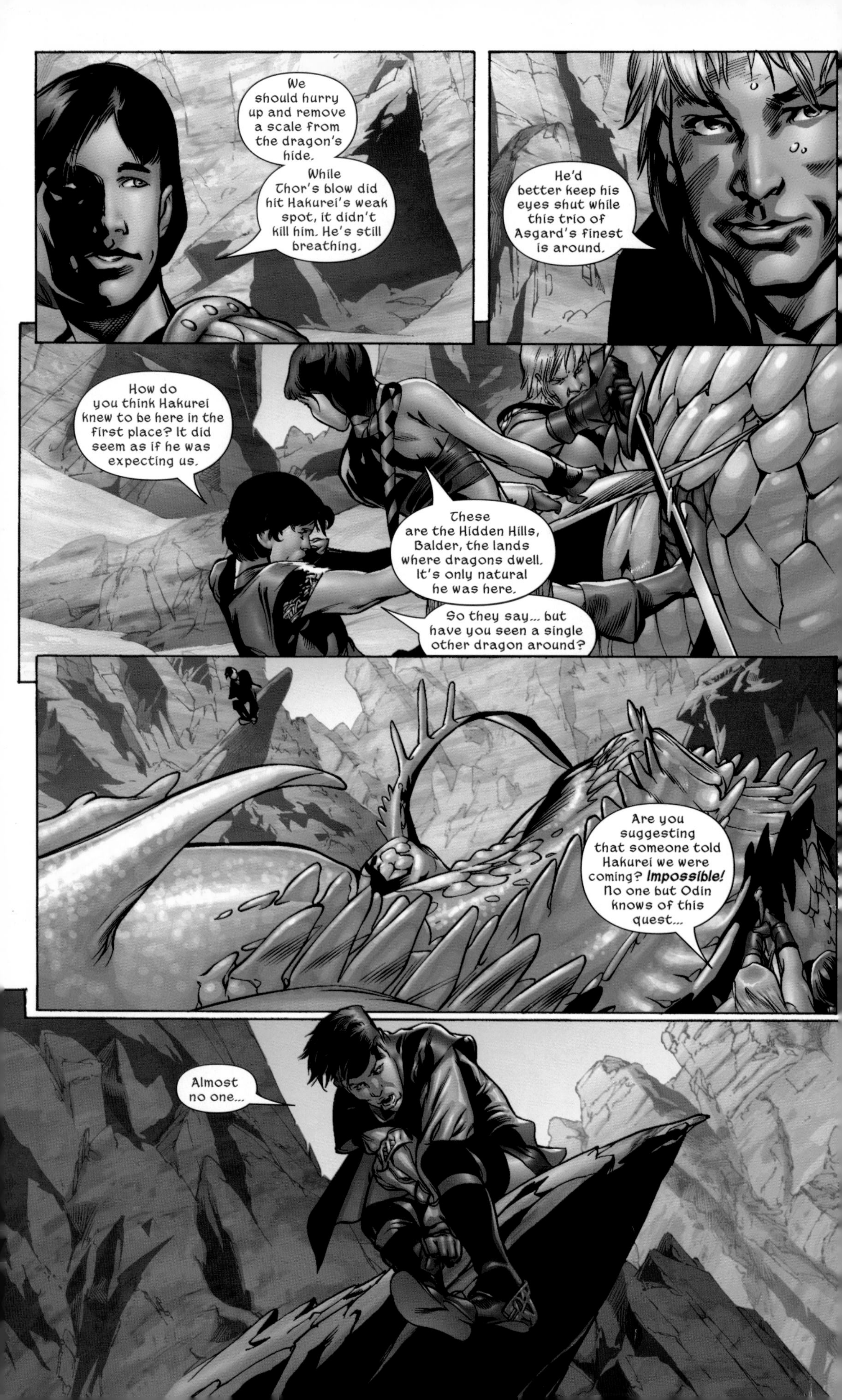
We should hurry up and remove a scale from the dragon's hide.
While Thor's blow did hit Hakurei's weak spot, it didn't kill him. He's still breathing.
He'd better keep his eyes shut while this trio of Asgard's finest is around.
How do you think Hakurei knew to be here in the first place? It did seem as if he was expecting us.
These are the Hidden Hills, Balder, the lands where dragons dwell. It's only natural he was here.
So they say... but have you seen a single other dragon around?
Are you suggesting that someone told Hakurei we were coming? Impossible! No one but Odin knows of this quest...
Almost no one...

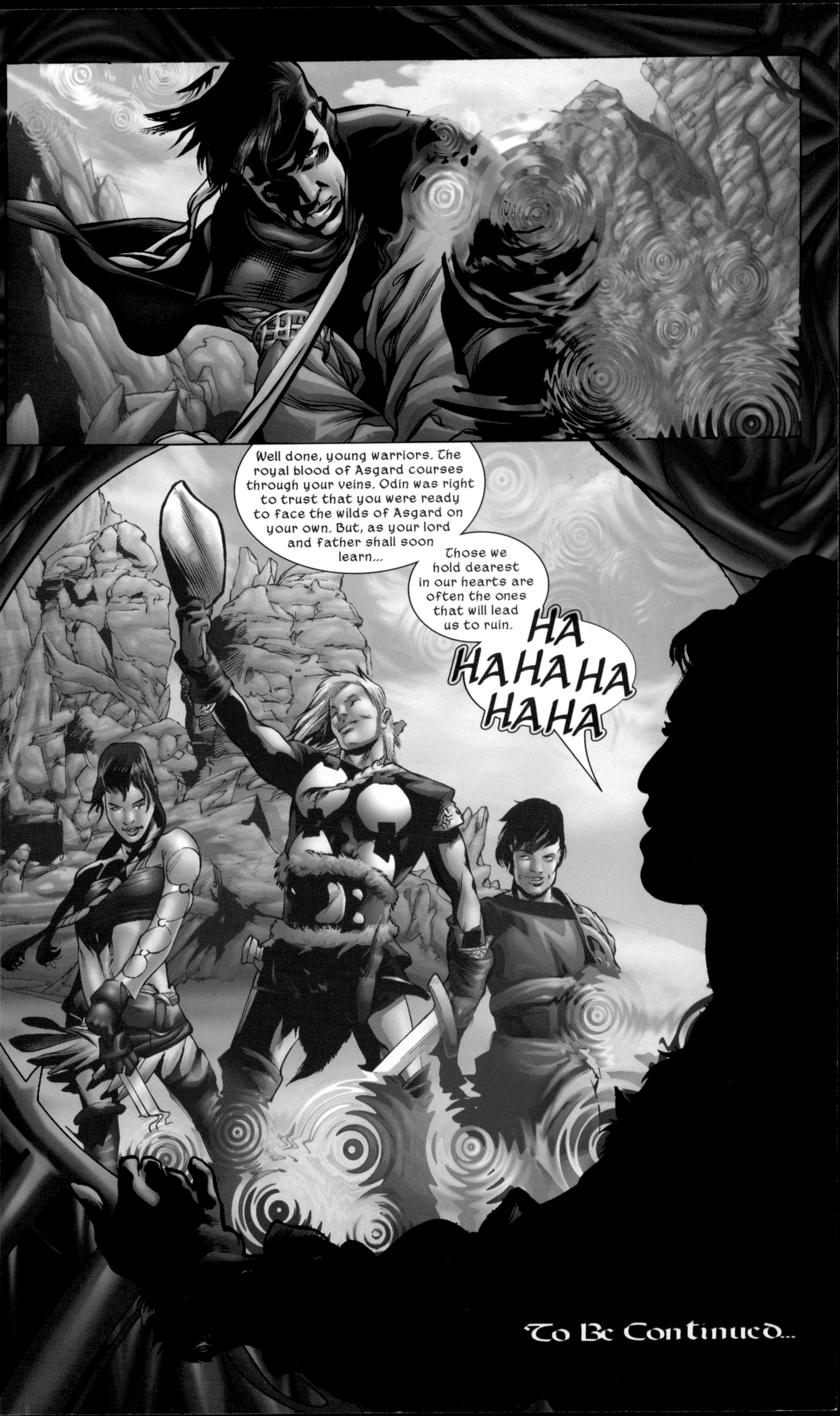
Well done, young warriors. The royal blood of Asgard courses through your veins. Odin was right to trust that you were ready to face the wilds of Asgard on your own. But, as your lord and father shall soon learn...
Those we hold dearest in our hearts are often the ones that will lead us to ruin.
HA HAHAHA HAHA
To Be Continued...

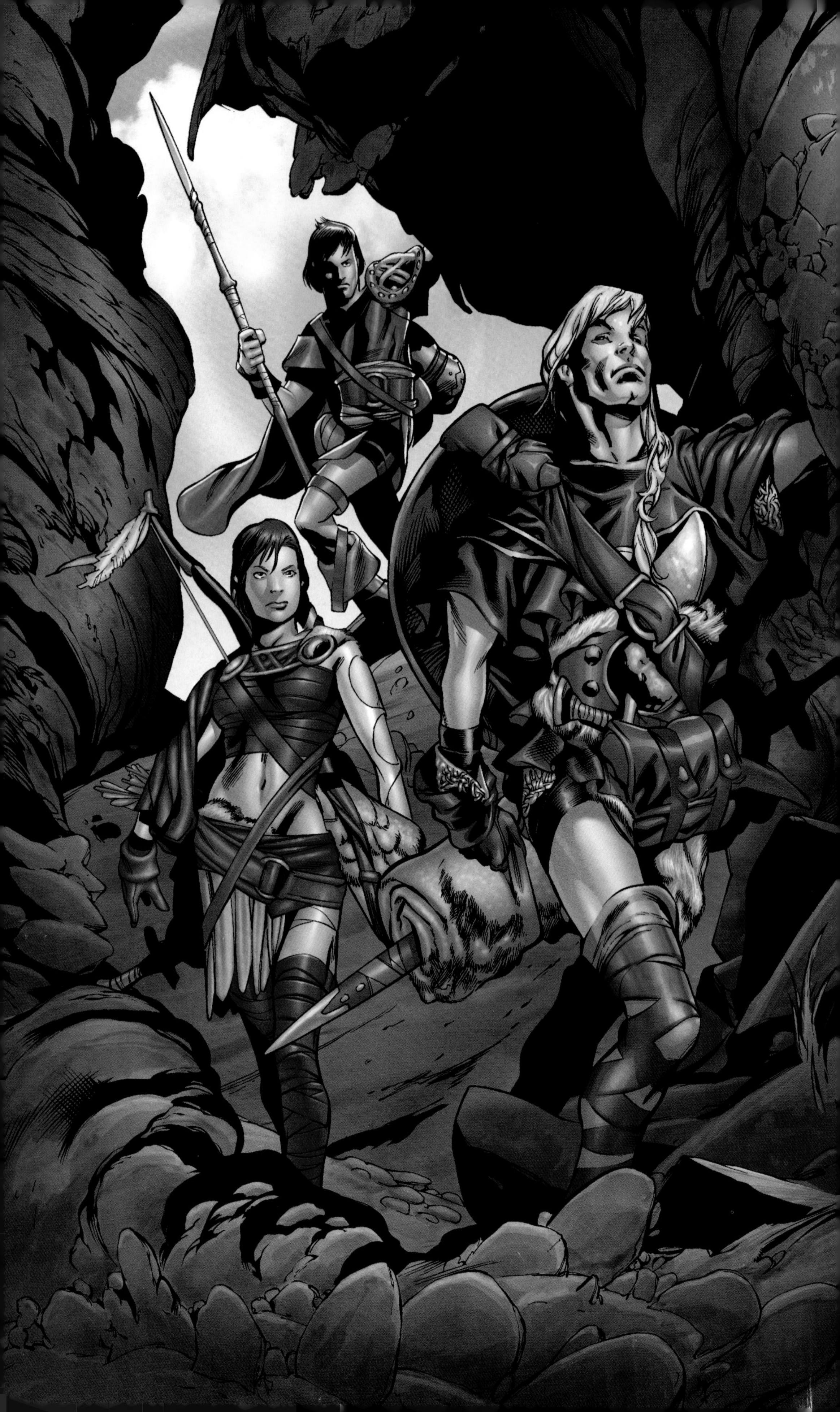